Via Lucis

In the Presence of Saint Joseph

Jerry Francis

About the Cover Art
Artist Jerry Francis
The Man in the Moon Watching Us
Private collection of Jerry Francis

Many of my paintings depict Divinity becoming visible in the ordinary, especially when viewing nature's scenery. My paintings attempt to express the reality of how I feel in the beauty in front of me and my prayerful gratitude. I mingle abstract art with a touch of the nearly invisible presence of Divinity. This book cover painting came to life when I was on vacation with my wife at a cabin overlooking a pond. It was mid-afternoon, and I had just watched the scene before me through the reflection on the pond's mirror-like surface.

The clouds drifted by to expose a perfect blue sky with what I thought was a small cloud. Looking up through the draping trees, I saw a brightly lit partial moon shining through the tree canopy. I lost myself in recognizing Divinity's involvement in this particular nature scene. Earlier that day, in the early morning light, I had been working on the book and had Saint Joseph still in the back of my mind.

The man on the moon watching us and how my mind and heart work was a metaphor for Saint Joseph and others in heaven doing the same. I could not resist setting the scene in the painting like a stage.

The moment I painted the reflecting light of the waxing half-moon, I knew the title and subtitle of this book. Via Lucis – The Way of Light, In the Presence of Saint Joseph.

Taking it one step further, I have Saint Joseph viewing the watercolor paintings of James Tissot scenes with us like we might in a stage performance. Imagine you are with Saint Joseph as he fictitiously comments on Jesus's various moments after His Resurrection. Feel free to have a fictitious conversation with him.

Other Artwork Used Within This Book

DEDICATION

I dedicate this book to everyone who enjoys seeing an artist's interpretation of a scene from Scripture.
Reflecting on faith-based art is a form of prayer.
We all appreciate your thoughts and prayers.

Acknowledgment

This book was made possible from a conversation with (and encouragement to write about it by) Paula H. regarding what Saint Joseph would think about the risen Jesus during Easter through Ascension inspired this *Via Lucis - The Way of Light, In the Presence of Saint Joseph.*

Table of Contents

Via Lucis Overview

The Via Lucis prayer is also known as the Way of Light and the Stations of Resurrection. The Via Lucis celebrates and highlights the most glorious time in the Christian liturgical year, the fifty days from Easter to Pentecost. An ancient inscription on the San Callisto Catacombs wall on the Appian Way in Rome inspired the idea for depicting the Way of Light. Praying the Via Lucis is becoming a modern interpretation of highlighting the continuing presence of the risen Lord. Scripture from the Gospel and Acts form reflection waypoints in the reality of Jesus's journey after the Cross. The Prayer with Jesus within the Via Lucis was reintroduced in the official Vatican prayer book for the Jubilee Year 2000 titled *Pilgrim Prayers*.[1] I have reviewed, consulted, and prayed this specific Via Lucis with friends from several Christian denominations. They find this enriches their beliefs.

The structure of the original Via Lucis is partially modeled on the prayer of Stations of the Cross. The Stations of the Cross vary by artist who each interprets and renders the scenes of the Passion of Christ. Stations of the Cross can be interpreted differently by different Christian faiths. However, I have ensured that all the scenes in this Via Lucis use the New Revised Standard Version Updated Edition of the Bible. Various artists have created sculptures and paintings after the Passion up to His Resurrection to remind us of the critical moments of

---

[1] Paraphrased portions from the Catholic News Agency https://www.catholicnewsagency.com

His Passion. For this Via Lucis, you can choose an artist who speaks to you about the scripture scene depicting Jesus's Resurrection through Ascension. I have selected the watercolor art of James Tissot since I admired his details when I acquired a pictorial Bible from the 1950s.

I also like James Tissot's striking watercolors because of his Christian transformation story. During a pilgrimage to Palestine in 1899, Tissot felt transported to the actual moments of Biblical events. Some say he had visions, but it is more realistic to see that in his grieving and the silence, grounded and using practical ways, he envisioned he was there in each scene of the New Testament. Each of Tissot's paintings speaks a thousand words in their vivid portrayals. His biography of feeling present in the historical scene was another reason I used his watercolors in this Via Lucis. One final reason for using his work is his ability to transcend various religious beliefs. After completing over three hundred scenes from the New Testament, Tissot used Hebrew materials, including Hebrew Scriptures, to paint another three hundred Illustrations. Tissot's Hebrew illustrations are owned and managed by the Jewish Museum in NYC.

Via Lucis - In the Presence of Saint Joseph

This Via Lucis version embraces the notion that Saint Joseph was spiritually in the fullness of heaven at the moment of Jesus's sacrifice. Because Saint Joseph was in heaven, he was also spiritually and eternally present with Jesus in the weeks following Christ's death on the Cross. This Via Lucis allows you to imagine what is happening by including the artistic scene. If you can imagine one step further, Joseph invites you to see and feel through his eyes. I describe the combination of Scripture, my interpretation of Saint Joseph, and the James Tissot painting as an encounter. There are eighteen such encounters in the book.

Another option is to consider that he is conversing with you, or perhaps you are just listening to your potential thoughts as you stand next to him. What I am suggesting is no different from the classic way any author uses words to let you see through a main character in a book. From this perspective, we can do the same in this Via Lucis with Saint Joseph.

The artist's scenes in this book let us imagine we are momentarily observing the living Christ. Even as a child, I have wanted Joseph to say something in Scripture. While he is silent in Scripture, he is not in his actions. As an author, I have taken liberties and artistic license in this Via Lucis with what I think Saint Joseph could tell us about his feelings.

I wish to be clear that these are concrete, grounded thoughts of what he could have said. The words and thoughts did not come from a mystical experience. However, they were inspired by deep prayer as I read the Scripture and viewed and reflected on each scene. I invite you to consider your or your group's thoughts as if you were together with Joseph. I have used this specific Via Lucis with my church community in this way, and it is beautiful to hear what others' inspired thoughts might be.

This book is not a devotion to Saint Joseph or meant to be mystical. However, we can ask our loved ones in heaven and people close to Jesus, such as Saint Joseph, to be prayer partners. As the husband of Mary, Saint Joseph, with the entire community of those in heaven, participates in the eternal journey with Jesus. We can reach out to any of them and ask them or anyone we ~~you~~ know in heaven to pray with us ~~you~~.

We have unique gifts that God has placed in our hearts and minds. We are called to ministry in some way. For me, ministry has a significant range of meanings. At one end of the spectrum are one-on-one situations, such as serving the needs of a single person or working hard to keep a relationship strong. As Christians, there are also more physical, outbound-oriented ministries, such as helping serve the local community's needs and global situations, including social justice initiatives. Prayer groups are a compelling way of learning, expressing, and living the language of our faith. I have spent more than two decades practicing and attempting to be in the presence of others and have witnessed incredible growth within myself and others through such groups.

The Via Lucis prayer focuses on why we are Christians because there would not be Christianity without the Resurrection. This book attempts to look at the Resurrection through many lenses so we may see and feel the Word in multiple dimensions. Doing so allows us to have more spiritual information than we already have. Seeing and hearing other people's thoughts gives us a greater understanding of the depth and breadth of God's works.

The format in the book provides multiple ways to experience our relationship with each other. It can also show us how much Jesus loves us through the dynamics and discussions with each other. A very short meditation in each of the eighteen encounters is an added dimension with which one can prepare for, explore, and focus on the discussions.

Generalized Christian Meditation

Concentrating on prayer for any prolonged period is complex and sometimes requires preparation. There are many meditation styles, some significantly contributing to Christian prayer. The meditation techniques in this book only focus on grounded Christian meditation types that do not cause someone to leave behind their thoughts and self. The meditations within are short forms that can relax your mind and body enough to be used to open the door to peace and then prayer.

I have been using Christian meditation daily for almost twenty 20 years. I find the premise of most meditation techniques intriguing, but I take a cautious approach with the ones when the goal is meditation without prayer. I believe there is a place for non-prayer-based meditations, as they can help bring peace to your mind. It is relatively easy to use the parts of these meditations that can calm our minds, so our hearts become open to prayer. When I find a meditation technique that may go well with prayer, I carve out the parts supporting the notion that we are both human and divine. I am passionate about believing God wants us to mingle our humanity and Divinity and never separate them.

The following is a series of brief descriptions of meditation techniques I have tried before prayer to get myself in the correct mindset. I also use them after prayer for reflection I have also adjusted meditation techniques to be more Christian-orientated. I have been sharing and using these techniques in group settings for over a decade. These techniques are preparatory or reflective and structured to provide relaxation, peace, and prayer before group discussion. These ideas may encourage you to explore other meditation styles. Almost any meditation style can be adjusted to become closer to your Christian values to work for you.

When choosing a meditation style, it is my view that we should not have to use a mind-altering substance to feel close to God. No doubt, our mind mixed with the substance creates a wonderous feeling. However, in these states of mind, Divinity is not working with us because our mind is not within our control. I believe our mind, body, and soul must be whole to blend with Divinity.

Some meditation techniques, even if short, can make us feel so relaxed that we fall into a type of daydream. This is especially true if meditation is used towards the end of our day. During this partial sleep-like state, it can feel that everything is right with the world. If that happens to you or someone in your group, accept that you have fallen asleep. When you awaken with feelings of joy, comfort, peace, and love, that is wonderful. This ability to wake up quickly is a sign that with the mingling of humanity and the divine, your humanity is still active.

The meditation techniques listed below can be used before or after prayer and complement the Via Lucis encounters within this book. If your group is already relaxed enough before you begin an encounter without meditation, you could consider saving the meditation afterward. It can also be used for reflection before a discussion to let people absorb what they have heard or read. If meditation is used before starting an encounter, you can also use meditation at the end.

If you like more than one of the meditation techniques, feel free to combine them. I have combined techniques many times when leading a group. I also use techniques that a specific group is comfortable with ~~and not forced.~~ It may make sense for your group to stick with a single approach. From my experience, I know it can take a few different styles until everyone in the group is satisfied. Group meditation, like many things in life, does require compromise and sometimes a reduction or tweak as necessary. The techniques below are some that I have found to be effective in a group format, given the variables of group dynamics. You will likely have to experiment to find one or more that works for your situation.

These techniques do fit under the meditation concept but are typically used for under a minute to help focus your heart and mind on God. You may recognize some of the techniques in this book as the starting points to variations of classic meditations. Others may be new to you because I created my own methods to reach peace in my heart. As a group leader, you may not be able to personally use one of these techniques because it is more important that you pay attention and be aware of your group's readiness to end the meditation time. I have had groups quickly adapt, and I was able to participate in the meditation partially. Any of these meditations may work in your group, but there is nothing wrong with experimenting when it comes to feeling like you are in the presence of God. There are six techniques used three times throughout the eighteen encounters.

1. Reduce Information Processing

One of the simplest forms of meditation is to place yourself in God's presence by pushing aside mental distractions. This is easier said than done, as there are always distractions. One way to think about this is to divide those parts of yourself into the things you must think about than those which are automatic. For instance, you do not have to think about your breathing. But, if you want to sit in a chair, a lot of information must be processed before you are seated. You may not notice it, but you have to slow down or even stop enough processing of what you are thinking about to be able to sit.

2. Relaxed and Comfortable Body Position

Amazingly, our body has to be comfortable and relaxed for more profound prayer techniques, because our body is a distraction. This is even more difficult in a group sitting around a table or open space. You may know your relaxed position but prefer not to show it to someone. The point of suitable meditation is to open up some space in yourself to let God surface from within. If you can get your body comfortable and relaxed, even partially, it creates space for God.

3. Reduce but Do Not Ignore Your Senses

Our senses are an essential part of who we are as humans. They can positively and negatively affect our well-being. The question we read about or hear regarding meditation or prayer is whether the senses should be ignored or shut off. I believe our senses and feelings are included in Genesis as we are made in God's likeness.

4. Remembering an Intense Non-Romantic Love Experience

I believe this is the absolute best form of Christian meditation. Each group member reflects on something or someone in their life that has deeply touched their soul. If you are the group leader, then you must be sensitive and observe that each person has completed thinking about these special moments that are entirely platonic. Each person holds the memory in their heart and does not have to share it with the group.

5. Reimagining

Every day, we all have something we wish would have gone another way. Reimagining something small that could have had a better result can be highly relaxing. This technique does not work for situations that include anger or someone being hurt. Before you start, say hello to God in your usual way. This is to acknowledge that you want God to see what you would have changed. Think about something small that you can see differently and stay in that moment long enough to taste the difference. You may be quite surprised how much joy and comfort it brings to your heart.

6. Open Your Bible to a Random Page

Open your Bible without thinking about what page you are going to see. Since an average Bible has far more Old Testament content than the New Testament, you are likelier to end up in the Old Testament. Read the whole paragraph that your eyes took you to. You will likely find something in that paragraph that resonates or intrigues you. Close your Bible and put it on your lap, resting your hands on it. Close your eyes and try not to let distractions get in the way of thinking about that paragraph.

Remember that these short meditation techniques may not work for you, or the mentioned types may not resonate. Do not feel you should ever be forced to use meditation; if it does not bring peace and comfort, it may not have value. God makes us unique, and I am only offering my experiences of quickly getting myself ready to concentrate on God. I offer this idea to do so as an option, not a requirement.

Suggested Approaches for Praying This Via Lucis

While we do not know much about Saint Joseph, we do know that his journey with Jesus began even before Jesus was born. Saint Joseph's lifetime encounter most likely remained similar throughout his encounter with Jesus. The only other person with more experience is Jesus's mother, Mary. If possible, in memory of the journey and passing into heaven of Jesus's human parents, you could consider not setting a time limit as you imagine yourself for each scene.

God wants you whole in mind, body, and soul and will not take away but only add to your nature. In grounded ways, God leverages our nature to express His joy so we may pass it on. This means your time in prayer does not require you to be devoid of everything into nothingness. As an amateur Christian scholar, I believe Jesus is concrete, with us now and incrementally working with us over time, building on who we are. This Via Lucis has the same feeling as the period examined, which does not happen in one instant but over the many weeks from Resurrection through Ascension. This period means a Via Lucis does not have to be like a single meal but rather tasted over many meals.

This Via Lucis has eighteen encounters, so you can use the classic Christian six-week period learning in three cycles. Another approach is to space the scenes to complete this Via Lucis over fifty days from Jesus's Resurrection to Ascension.

Other General Via Lucis Options and Guidance

This Via Lucis is structured to provide the ability to adapt to your situation. For instance, in the silent portions of this Via Lucis, you can also consider substituting what a different imagined holy person might say. I am sure Saint Joseph would be quite joyful if you could select someone from Scripture or even a holy person you know. I suggest you keep the conversation spiritual and concrete no matter who you pray with. With a prayer like Via Lucis, these multiple modalities help understand the mystery of reading Scripture or listening to a sermon.

With the quiet time in prayers such as a Via Lucis, it is perfectly natural and acceptable to feel totally at peace and relaxed. Mixing the divine and human using a Via Lucis prayer is as ancient as Scripture, allowing us to sense the reality of God wherever we may be. If you become comfortable with prayer techniques like a Via Lucis, thinking this way can become second nature without requiring specific or long prayer time. Paraphrasing Saint Paul, we can decrease so He can increase.

He who has the bride is the bridegroom. The friend of the bridegroom, who stands and hears him, rejoices greatly at the bridegroom's voice. For this reason, my joy has been fulfilled. He must increase, but I must decrease (John 3:29-30).

Living for God in Christ Jesus - Opening Preparation
First Encounter with Saint Joseph

Reading:

For if we have grown into union with him through a death like his, we shall also be united with him in the Resurrection. We know that our old self was crucified with him, so that our sinful body might be done away with, that we might no longer be in slavery to sin. For a dead person has been absolved from sin. If, then, we have died with Christ, we believe that we shall also live with him. We know that Christ, raised from the dead, dies no more; death no longer has power over him. As to his death, he died to sin once and for all; as to his life, he lives for God. Consequently, you too must think of yourselves as [being] dead to sin and living for God in Christ Jesus. (Romans 6:5-11)

Reflection:

Let us pray with others we know in heaven and Saint Joseph and upon the Resurrection through the Ascension of Christ and discover the pathway of light that Jesus blazes through our lives.

15

The Anxiety of Saint Joseph by James Tissot[2]

Prayer

Jesus, open my heart as I encounter scenes of You in words, art, and imagination. In Jesus' name, Amen.

Meditation Technique: Reduce Information Processing

The basic concept of this technique is to put aside those technical distractions in your mind that are stopping you from becoming present with God. We can use the control of breathing as a quick reminder of how to begin. For a minute, try to stop automatic breathing and take a few breaths at ten-second intervals. Now, think of your relationship with God. A major issue for peace for most of us is all the information processing and thoughts about things we need to do going on in our heads. We can use the same technique as breathing to pick off each thing that may need processing. Take a breath, and during that breath, let one of those things that seem to be necessary or that you have to deal with come to the surface.

---

[2] James Tissot (Nantes, France, 1836–1902, Chenecey-Buillon, France). *The Anxiety of Saint Joseph (L'anxiété de Saint Joseph)*, 1886-1894. Opaque watercolor over graphite on gray wove paper, Image: 6 5/16 x 7 13/16 in. (16 x 19.8 cm). Brooklyn Museum, Purchased by public subscription, 00.159.20 (Photo: Brooklyn Museum, 00.159.20_PS2.jpg) - https://www.brooklynmuseum.org/opencollection/objects/4426

Assure yourself you will think about it later and not now. Keep doing this routine until your mind is settled. Peace will arrive if you can push aside a few things for later. During your discussion period, if one of these items you tried to push aside comes to mind, take a controlled breath and assure yourself you will get to it later. This meditation technique is constant and should give you an opportunity to come back into the presence of the waiting arms of God.

Discussion Group Scenario:

What does prayer with those you know in heaven or Saint Joseph mean to you? Are you comfortable with praying with someone who has passed? Is anyone in the group willing to share their thoughts on this style of praying?

The Resurrection

Second Encounter with Saint Joseph

All: We adore You, O Christ, and we praise You! Because by the Wood of the Cross and the Light of the Resurrection, You have redeemed the world!

Reading: *And suddenly there was a great earthquake, for an angel of the Lord, descending from heaven, came and rolled back the stone and sat on it. His appearance was like lightning and his clothing white as snow. For fear of him the guards shook and became like dead men.* (Matthew 28:2-5).

Saint Joseph: Brothers and Sisters, sometimes the extraordinary is necessary to convince someone that Jesus was here as God. My Son had to appear to those surrounding the tomb, as many were non-believers. You can encounter my Son with the stories of Jesus written down in Scripture. Many of you can see the risen Jesus in the eyes and expressions of love and compassion of those surrounding you. I pray with you for the gift of not needing the extraordinary as you witness the wonder of my risen Son throughout your day.

19

The Resurrection by James J. Tissot [3]

Prayer: Saint Joseph, humble servant of our Lord Jesus Christ, pray with us. In Jesus' name, Amen.

Meditation Technique: Relaxed and Comfortable Body Position

Supporting the weight of various parts of your body can be quite relaxing and meditative, as that is how a bed works to let us fall asleep. In the privacy of your home, in addition to your bed, you probably have comfortable seating and positions that reduce discomfort. However, doing so is impractical in most group settings. In a discussion group, we sit more conventionally supported in a chair. In the silence in the room, try to concentrate on discovering the parts of your body that are giving you discomfort.

Our mind can cooperate with our struggles if we let it do so. Think about the techniques of how you convince yourself to do something you do not want to do. This same process can also be leveraged for relaxation. As you mentally uncover each discomfort, work with your mind to relax that part of your body. Think about the idea that each discomfort is only

---

[3] James Tissot (French, 1836-1902). TOUCH ME NOT (NOLI ME TANGERE), 1886-1894. Opaque watercolor over graphite on gray wove paper, Image: 11 1/8 x 7 1/2 in. (28.3 x 19.1 cm). Brooklyn Museum, Purchased by public subscription, 00.159.335 (Photo: Brooklyn Museum, 00.159.335_PS2.jpg) https://www.brooklynmuseum.org/opencollection/objects/4611

temporary. Can you hold it at bay so you can think about the encounter and discussion instead? It is okay to repeat the process at any point until there is peace in your body.

Discussion Group Scenario:

Imagine yourself wanting to believe in Jesus, but you are not quite all the way there yet. You are given the opportunity to stand in front of the unopened tomb, not knowing what to think. Suddenly, the boulder before the tomb moves to the side, and Jesus rises before you. You witness non-believers falling asleep before they get a chance to see Jesus. Re-read Matthew 28:2-5. Allow yourself to downplay the extraordinary of what you have seen. Why did you not fall asleep like the others around you? Now that you know why you are not asleep, is your belief stronger? Why or why not?

Jesus Rises from the Dead

Third Encounter with Saint Joseph

All: We adore You, O Christ, and we praise You! Because by the Wood of the Cross and the Light of the Resurrection, You have redeemed the world!

Reading: *Then the angel said to the women in reply, "Do not be afraid! I know that you are seeking Jesus the crucified. He is not here, for he has been raised just as he said. Come and see the place where he lay.* (Matthew 28:5-6)

Saint Joseph: Sister, I was visited by an angel like you, forever removing all my fears. God's Grace filled me with love, faith, and hope to be the human father of Jesus and devoted spouse of Mary. Allow your heart to be united with ours, rise with us, and join the affirmation of our love. Without fear, walk with me into the presence of your Brother.

23

Mary Magdalene Questions the Angels in the Tomb by James Tissot[4]

Prayer: Saint Joseph, husband of Mary and fearless protector of the Mystical Body of Christ, pray with us. In Jesus' name, Amen.

Meditation Technique: Reduce but Do Not Ignore Your Senses

If you had Covid in the last few years, you may have been deprived of the sense of taste. Some drugs for cancer can create the same condition. Some people are born without sight or the ability to hear. For instance, I was overwhelmed when, in my forties, I heard better by wearing hearing aids for the first time. I had to take them out and introduce myself to better hearing over time. My hearing improved for reasons I do not know, and now I only occasionally need aids.

God gives us the capacity to use our senses to enjoy time with Him. One option we can use to focus our attention on God is to quiet one of our senses. Many people have learned to unconsciously close their eyes to pray. This allows the space created by removing the activities within our sight to be filled with God's love. This simple practice of quieting a sense may bring peace and calm to open your heart to a lively conversation.

---

[4] James Tissot (French, 1836-1902). MARY MAGDALENE QUESTIONS THE ANGELS IN THE TOMB (MADELEINE DANS LE TOMBEAU INTERROGE LES ANGES), 1886-1894. Opaque watercolor over graphite on gray wove paper, Image: 7 1/4 x 5 3/4 in. (18.4 x 14.6 cm). Brooklyn Museum, Purchased by public subscription, 00.159.333 (Photo: Brooklyn Museum, 00.159.333_PS2.jpg)https://www.brooklynmuseum.org/opencollection/objects/13521

Discussion Group Scenario:

Imagine you are there with the women, the angel, and Saint Joseph at the open tomb. Saint Joseph has started a conversation with you. What thoughts or questions do you share with Saint Joseph, the women, or the angel?

The Disciples Discover the Empty Tomb

Fourth Encounter with Saint Joseph

All: We adore You, O Christ, and we praise You! Because by the Wood of the Cross and the Light of the Resurrection, You have redeemed the world!

Reading: *Then the other disciple also went in, the one who had arrived at the tomb first, and he saw and believed.* (John 20:28).

St. Joseph: In the witness of Mary's empty womb, I humbly offered myself to our Lord in adopted fatherhood. God has given you this same precious gift of faith to seek the risen Christ. You can remember that the tomb is empty because Christ is with the living. With open minds and eyes, you already know Him in the Word, the breaking of bread, and the gift of love to others. Believe that even in your empty and lonely places, Mary and I are also with you. In the silence of your heart, know that the Lord reveals His great love for you.

V

27

Saint Peter and Saint John Run to the Sepulcher by James Tissot[5]

Prayer: Saint Joseph, humble, brave, obedient, and loyal, pray with us. In Jesus's name, Amen

Meditation Technique: Remembering an Intense Non-Romantic Love Experience
It may sound odd, but I believe this is the absolute best form of Christian meditation. There is pure joy in being happy because a friend or child has said or done something for or with you that you recognize as beyond the ordinary. It can be so intense that you feel your heart leaping like Elizabeth with Mary. To give you an example of what I mean, here is one of my personal favorites.

I was in my late teens fishing at night at a remote pond almost a mile into a forest. I had brought a flashlight, but the moonlight was especially bright enough to see. I was sitting on the sand on the small beach and had just put a small bell at the tip of my rod to hear if a fish was biting.

---

[5] James Tissot (French, 1836-1902). SAINT PETER AND SAINT JOHN RUN TO THE SEPULCHRE (SAINT PIERRE ET SAINT JEAN COURENT AU SÉPULCRE), 1886-1894. Opaque watercolor over graphite on gray wove paper, Image: 8 3/16 x 6 1/8 in. (20.8 x 15.6 cm). Brooklyn Museum, Purchased by public subscription, 00.159.332 (Photo: Brooklyn Museum, 00.159.332_PS2.jpg) https://www.brooklynmuseum.org/opencollection/objects/13520

Suddenly, a man dressed in white came out of the trail onto the beach. I did not even hear him. I could see his smile in the moonlight while he said a few words: "I thought you were a rock." He walked by me and then looped back to the side of the beach, where the return trail led to the parking lot.

I was so stunned at the love I felt at that moment that I could not say anything back. To this day, this experience causes me to believe that a stranger was telling me that love would allow me to focus on being in tune with what God wants. It took me a couple of days to realize I was to be like Peter in my rock of faith. As of that point in my life, it was the most intense but grounded experience of someone loving me in a way I had not known.

Perhaps I make too much of this experience. However, it frequently comes to mind, and I am instantly at peace within a minute. I believe this man wanted me to learn that instant, intense non-romantic is possible. Take a moment to relax and meditate on one of your stories that brings you this sense of love to open the space for God's love to be present.

Discussion Group Scenario:

When some hear the passage, "*Then the other disciple also went in, the one who had arrived at the tomb first, and he saw and believed,*" it could potentially indicate that the other disciple did not believe in Jesus or that He has risen to heaven. However, Scripture infers far more because Jesus has risen in our hearts. What does Jesus-within-you mean to you? How do you explain that to someone? Same question, but the Holy Spirit or the Father?

Draw your thoughts so far

The Risen Lord Appears to Mary Magdalene

Fifth Encounter with Saint Joseph

All: We adore You, O Christ, and we praise You! Because by the Wood of the Cross and the Light of the Resurrection, You have redeemed the world!

Reading: *'Woman, why are you weeping? Whom are you looking for?' She thought it was the gardener and said to him, 'Sir, if you carried him away, tell me where you laid him, and I will take him.' Jesus said to her, 'Mary!' She turned and said to him in Hebrew, 'Rabbouni,' which means Teacher. Jesus said to her, 'Do not touch me, because I have not yet ascended to the Father. But go to my brothers and say to them, 'I am ascending to my Father and your Father, to my God and your God.'* (John 20:14b-17).

Saint Joseph: As a child, I held my Son's hands as we shaped pieces of wood into perfection. He grew strong and independent, taking wings before my eyes. In mingling our love for each other, I began to understand humility. To hear him call me Dad would send graces in overwhelming shivers; how could I not love back? I can hear Him calling you by name, to love back, to go to your brothers and sisters. Let go of what holds you back, take wings, and tell the world you have seen the risen Lord.

33

Touch Me Not by James J. Tissot[6]

Prayer: Saint Joseph, humble servant of our Lord Jesus Christ, pray with us. In Jesus' name, Amen

Meditation Technique: Reimagining

Every day, we all have something that could have gone another way. It can be extremely relaxing to reimagine something small and insignificant that could have had a different result. This technique can bring a smile and lift you up to see options. Notice I am not suggesting a better result. Before you start, say hello to God in your usual way. This is to acknowledge that you want God to see you appreciate the gift of change.

For instance, I have painted several hundred abstract faith-oriented paintings. The ones that intrigue me the most are when I paint the Cross. Almost every time after I have completed one, I think about what I might change the next time. It gives me great comfort in thinking that the possibilities are endless, and that spills over whenever I have something happen that could have been different.

---

[6] James Tissot (French, 1836-1902). TOUCH ME NOT (NOLI ME TANGERE), 1886-1894. Opaque watercolor over graphite on gray wove paper, Image: 11 1/8 x 7 1/2 in. (28.3 x 19.1 cm). Brooklyn Museum, Purchased by public subscription, 00.159.335 (Photo: Brooklyn Museum, 00.159.335_PS2.jpg)https://www.brooklynmuseum.org/opencollection/objects/4611

Think about something small that you can see differently and stay in that moment long enough to taste the difference. You may be quite surprised how much joy and comfort it brings to your heart. Over the years, I have used this technique for more complicated situations, and the calming effect energizes me for more profound prayer.

Discussion Group Scenario:

You may have experienced a sudden situation of someone you have not seen someone in many years. Something has changed in that person, and you do not recognize them. How long did it take you to put the changes aside and know who it was. Perhaps they sensed you did not know who they were, and they mentioned enough clues for you to know who they were. How did you react. How would you feel if you were Mary, not recognizing Jesus, then when you do He tells you not to touch Him.

Draw a picture of Jesus calling your name

The Risen Lord Appears on the Road to Emmaus

Sixth Encounter with Saint Joseph

All: We adore You, O Christ, and we praise You! Because by the Wood of the Cross and the Light of the Resurrection, You have redeemed the world!

Reading: *Now that very day two of them were going to a village seven miles from Jerusalem called Emmaus, and they were conversing about all the things that had occurred. And it happened that while they were conversing and debating, Jesus himself drew near and walked with them, but their eyes were prevented from recognizing him. He asked them, 'What are you discussing as you walk along?' They stopped, looking downcast. One of them, named Cleopas, said to him in reply, 'Are you the only visitor to Jerusalem who does not know of the things that have taken place there in these days?* (Luke 24:13-18)

Saint Joseph: Mary and I know your sense of despair and loss. We discovered it when we realized we were without our Son. We found him right where we should have known, inside His Father's house. As you sometimes do, we were at a loss and did not know where to find Jesus. We can help you seek joy and peace to overcome loss, suffering, and pain on your road. No matter where you are, the risen Lord is with you. Open your hearts like your friend Cleopas, and you will recognize Jesus is there.

Disciples on Their Way to Emmaus by James J. Tissot[7]

Prayer: Saint Joseph, pray with us for those who do not know Jesus. In Jesus' name, Amen

Meditation Technique: Open Your Bible to A Random Page

Since a normal Bible has far more Old Testament content than the New Testament, if you open the Bible, you are likelier to end up in the Old Testament. I just did so and opened to Johua 12:7-24 regarding all the kings Joshua defeated. As I read it, I did not have that immediate sense of comfort as it was not encouraging, and I almost put my writing this paragraph aside. However, when this happens, from experience I know I should reflect on it a little because I probably have not understood how God wants me to think about it. It did not take me long to realize the positive of defeating something that was bothering me. I instantly felt at ease and calm, to finish writing. This idea of finding the positives in any Scripture you read, can bring peace.

---

[7] James Tissot (French, 1836-1902). THE PILGRIMS OF EMMAUS ON THE ROAD (LES PÈLERINS D'EMMAÜS EN CHEMIN), 1886-1894. Opaque watercolor over graphite on gray wove paper, Image: 7 7/16 x 10 5/8 in. (18.9 x 27 cm). Brooklyn Museum, Purchased by public subscription, 00.159.338 (Photo: Brooklyn Museum, 00.159.338_PS1.jpg)
https://www.brooklynmuseum.org/opencollection/objects/13524

Discussion Group Scenario:

Some of you have felt the loss of a loved one and the sense of never touching and being with that person again. The closer the person was to you, the more angst you feel. It is yours personally, and no one can know the depth. You reached out to friends and family and to God. Did you think even God could not help? Was God to blame for a while? Did you turn to feel the outpouring of the risen Jesus' love?

Jesus Appears to Peter

Seventh Encounter with Saint Joseph

All: We adore You, O Christ, and we praise You! Because by the Wood of the Cross and the Light of the Resurrection, You have redeemed the world!

Reading: *So they set out at once and returned to Jerusalem where they found gathered together the eleven and those with them who were saying, "The Lord has truly been raised and has appeared to Simon!"* (Luke 24:33-34)

Saint Joseph: From Heaven I watched Peter, James, and John see Jesus standing in Glory near Moses and Elijah. I treasure this moment of pure holiness, human and Divinity, gathered with and around my Son. For Peter, for you, sometimes lost in loneliness, is to be blessed again by Jesus's Glorified presence. For Peter, faith became eternal, and nothing could stop his belief. Our Lord offers himself to you, appearing repeatedly in your heart. He is responding to your human needs with the glorious light of Divinity.

43

Apparition of Our Lord to Saint Peter by James Tissot [8]

Prayer: Saint Joseph, comforter of the troubled and lost, pray with us. In Jesus' name, Amen.

Meditation Technique: Reduce Information Processing

This book has six meditation techniques; select one you like or use one of your own. Feel free to return to the first one of reducing information processing techniques. This time, you could imagine a cell phone never existed, or you left it out of reach. Holding that thought means you are making time for God, so you can use that time to think of all the God-generated beauty surrounding you.

---

[8] James Tissot (French, 1836-1902). APPARITION OF OUR LORD TO SAINT PETER (APPARITION DE NOTRE-SEIGNEUR À ST-PIERRE), 1886-1894. Opaque watercolor over graphite on gray wove paper, Image: 11 1/2 x 7 15/16 in. (29.2 x 20.2 cm). Brooklyn Museum, Purchased by public subscription, 00.159.336 (Photo: Brooklyn Museum, 00.159.336_PS2.jpg)

Discussion Group Scenario:

In Scripture, we hear Peter witnessing Jesus in Resurrection and Glory with Moses and Elijah in the Transfiguration. Other disciples do not see Jesus as many times. Some of you have witnessed Jesus in your life in more than intense, average ways. Do you wonder why some people seem to have more faith? Can it be because they have more consolations of Jesus to get their attention? We hear very little of some disciples of Jesus in Scripture. What might be the reasons for this?

The Risen Lord Recognized at the Table

Eighth Encounter with Saint Joseph

All: We adore You, O Christ, and we praise You! Because by the Wood of the Cross and the Light of the Resurrection, You have redeemed the world!

Reading: *They urged Him, 'Stay with us, for it is nearly evening and the day is almost over.' So He went in to stay with them. And it happened that while He was with them at table, He took bread, said the blessing, broke it, and gave it to them. With that, their eyes were opened and they recognized Him, but He vanished from their sight. Then they said to each other, 'Were not our hearts burning within us while He spoke to us on the way and opened the scriptures to us.'* (Luke 24: 29-32)

Saint Joseph: Meals with our Son were filled with awe and wonder. As we listened to Him, grace entered and fed us, burning within us to share with others. I humbly placed His beauty into my craft, unique, like yours. When you break bread together, He sets you on fire with His love, giving you inner warmth. Return it to the world as you respond to humanity's physical and spiritual hunger pangs.

47

He Vanished from Their Sight by James Tissot[9]

Prayer: Saint Joseph, an example to workers, pray with us. In Jesus' name, Amen.

Meditation Technique: Relaxed and Comfortable Body Position

In the previous use of this technique, you experimented with talking yourself into thinking that whatever discomfort you had was temporary. You can try transferring the discomfort to another part of your body or gently pinching the skin between your thumb and pointer finger. If you have had physical therapy, you know that sometimes you have to have a little pain to make something better over the long term. You can try closing your eyes, imagining you are comfortable. The idea is to displace that discomfort so you can relax and have some quiet time with God before you start your discussion group to collect your thoughts.

---

[9]James Tissot (French, 1836-1902). HE VANISHED FROM THEIR SIGHT (IL DISPARUT À LEURS YEUX), 1886-1894. Opaque watercolor over graphite on gray wove paper, Image: 9 3/4 x 6 13/16 in. (24.8 x 17.3 cm). Brooklyn Museum, Purchased by public subscription, 00.159.339 (Photo: Brooklyn Museum, 00.159.339_PS2.jpg) https://www.brooklynmuseum.org/opencollection/objects/13525

Discussion Group Scenario:

If you are like most believers, Scripture burns equally in your heart each time you read from the Bible. We do not always recognize what the Word means to us in these moments. Have you had the experience of reading a passage and it just seemed to be there for you? Think about that: without warning, did it mean something? Doesn't Jesus do the same for the disciples by coming and going? Why do you think these Scripture insights come to you?

The Risen Lord Appears to the Community of Disciples

Ninth Encounter with Saint Joseph

All: We adore You, O Christ, and we praise You! Because by the Wood of the Cross and the Light of the Resurrection, You have redeemed the world!

Reading: *Then he said to them, 'Why are you troubled? And why do questions arise in your hearts? Look at My hands and My feet, that it is I Myself. Touch Me and see, because a ghost does not have flesh and bones as you can see I have, And as He said this, He showed them His hands and His feet.* (Luke 24: 38-40)

Saint Joseph: I know the wounds of humanity and the suffering of so many because of the birth of my Son. I watched as He was tortured, torn, penetrated. Evil's wickedness and jealousy of power brought darkness all around us. In victory, in God's absolute love, Christ's wounds were healed, their glorious light directly visible to His friends. Hold out your hands and give your wounds to God's love. Allow him to touch, heal, and transform your suffering into joy.

The Appearance of Christ in the Cenacle, James Tissot [10]

Prayer: With hope for the wounded, Saint Joseph, pray with us. In Jesus' name, Amen.

Meditation Technique: Reduce but Do Not Ignore Your Senses

When you want a quiet place to think, where do you go? It is someplace physical such as a walk in the woods, your church when you know no one is there, or perhaps tucked into a quiet spot of a library. Maybe you are lucky, and you find quiet even on a busy city street or a crowded meeting room. When we find these places of quiet, we are reducing the stimuli that surrounds us, and one of the most significant is sound. Finding a way that works for you to reduce the impact of sounds creates the opportunity to calm our mind to let warm thoughts enter. Right now, you may be in a group gathering. Everyone may be quiet in their own way, but there are still the surrounding sounds. Let these background noises dissipate. Appreciate that you have a group of people willing to help create the quiet. There is joy in that for everyone, let that group joy join your own to bring stillness to your mind.

---

[10] James Tissot (French, 1836-1902). THE APPEARANCE OF CHRIST AT THE CENACLE (APPARITION DU CHRIST AU CÉNACLE), 1886-1894. Opaque watercolor over graphite on gray wove paper, Image: 5 1/2 x 10 1/4 in. (14 x 26 cm). Brooklyn Museum, Purchased by public subscription, 00.159.340 (Photo: Brooklyn Museum, 00.159.340_PS2.jpg
https://www.brooklynmuseum.org/opencollection/objects/13526

Discussion Group Scenario:

We have all been wounded in some way, be it physical, emotional, or even spiritual. Some of you may have known people once filled with the Holy Spirit but because something deep happened to them, they seemed to lose their faith. Your prayers with them and words of encouragement seem lost to them. Jesus does the same with those in the upper room. He speaks to them, and then, in silence, He shows them the Glory blazing from His hands and feet. Have you tried just being present over and over again without words with someone who has been wounded? What was the result?

The Risen Lord Strengthens the Faith of Thomas

Tenth Encounter with Saint Joseph

All: We adore You, O Christ, and we praise You! Because by the Wood of the Cross and the Light of the Resurrection, You have redeemed the world!

Reading: *Thomas, called Didymus, one of the Twelve, was not with them when Jesus came. So the other disciples said to him, 'We have seen the Lord.' But he said to them, 'Unless I see the mark of the nails in his hands and put my finger into the nail marks and put my hand into his side, I will not believe.' Now a week later his disciples were again inside and Thomas was with them. Jesus came, although the doors were locked, and stood in their midst and said, 'Peace be with you' Then he said to Thomas, 'Put your finger here and see my hands, and bring your hand and put it into my side, and do not be unbelieving, but believe.'* (John 20: 24-29)

Saint Joseph: Imagine how I felt, a lowly carpenter asked to raise God. The same God I worshipped; how could this be? Yet, when I first held my Son, all doubt was gone. I knew my embrace would forever intertwine with Jesus. I smile when I think of how He shaped me into a human full of goodness so God, as Jesus, could experience man's potential. You are asked to do the same, examine and embrace Christ, and let Him embrace you. He is an eternal spring renewing you, making you a better person, so you, like Saint Thomas, might know and share your faith.

The Disbelief or Doubting of St. Thomas, James Tissot[11]

Prayer: Saint Joseph, a man of faith, pray with us. In Jesus' name, Amen.

Meditation Technique: Remembering an Intense Non-Romantic Love Scene

If you have participated in the birth of a child, it is one of the most intense feelings of love we can have. While we hold the baby, we feel our warmth flowing into the child. Touching the baby's soft skin and humming add to the scene. If you have not had this experience, ask someone who has to describe it for you. We can use this memory to bring us joy and peace. Let the memory of the experience bring a meditative smile to your face and rekindle the warmth in your heart.

.

---

[11] James Tissot (French, 1836-1902). THE DISBELIEF OF SAINT THOMAS (INCREDULITÉ DE SAINT THOMAS), 1886-1894. Opaque watercolor over graphite on gray wove paper, Image: 7 13/16 x 5 5/16 in. (19.8 x 13.5 cm). Brooklyn Museum, Purchased by public subscription, 00.159.341 (Photo: Brooklyn Museum, 00.159.341_PS2.jpg) - https://www.brooklynmuseum.org/opencollection/objects/4613

Discussion Group Scenario:

Why does Scripture give us a doubting Thomas? Don't we all know someone like that? This is especially true of specific career paths where data, results, and facts are always present in someone's life. Do you know someone who, despite being in one of these careers, is not a doubting Thomas or perhaps was one? Why, despite Thomas's beliefs, does Jesus gently convince him? Does the Holy Spirit work that way in your life?

Jesus Christ Appears on the Shore of Lake Tiberias

Eleventh Encounter with Saint Joseph

All: We adore You, O Christ, and we praise You! Because by the Wood of the Cross and the Light of the Resurrection, You have redeemed the world!

Reading: *After these things Jesus showed himself again to the disciples by the Sea of Tiberias, and he showed himself in this way. ² Gathered there together were Simon Peter, Thomas called the Twin, Nathanael of Cana in Galilee, the sons of Zebedee, and two others of his disciples. ³ Simon Peter said to them, "I am going fishing." They said to him, "We will go with you." They went out and got into the boat, but that night they caught nothing.* (John 21:1-3)

Saint Joseph: I worked hard in my workshop to support my family. It was difficult, as I depended on people buying what I built. My Son learned how to be a fine craftsman, to find and carve with the grain of the wood. I understood what God wanted from me: to help Jesus become skilled in exposing beauty before it was formed and be strong and confident. I was not surprised to see Him on the shore with His friends, telling them with certainty where the fish were. I can see His presence in your life. He knows you well, helping you know where to go and how to gently and confidently tell others about what He has done for you.

Jesus Christ Appears on the Shore of Lake Tiberius, James Tissot[12]

Prayer: Saint Joseph, lover of God and neighbor, pray with us. In Jesus' name, Amen.

Meditation Technique: Reimagining

There is a cornfield in the back of my house. I let the local farmer use an old dirt path to bring his equipment to work the field. I imagine the field is something else during different times of the yearly seasons. For instance, in the newness of spring, I imagine it is a beautiful small pond on which I can use a rowboat. If I struggle to focus on one of the other meditative techniques, I fall back to the cornfield. Viewing that field as a pond, a meadow filled with grazing sheep, or rows of flowers brings me great joy and peace. This technique does not have to be so glorious; something in your hand works just as well.

---

[12] James Tissot (French, 1836-1902). CHRIST APPEARS ON THE SHORE OF LAKE TIBERIAS (APPARITION DU CHRIST SUR LES BORDS DU LAC DE TIBÉRIADE), 1886-1894. Opaque watercolor over graphite on gray wove paper, Image: 5 7/8 x 9 1/16 in. (14.9 x 23 cm). Brooklyn Museum, Purchased by public subscription, 00.159.343 (Photo: Brooklyn Museum, 00.159.343_PS2.jpg)-
https://www.brooklynmuseum.org/opencollection/objects/4615

Discussion Group Scenario:

Jesus had spent considerable time with the Disciples, most of whom were fishermen. Jesus had previously sent out these same men to proclaim the Good New. They had already seen and talked to the Gloried Jesus, and we would expect them to react to those visits. However, we see them returning to their former lives. Why would that be? Shouldn't they be out continuing to evangelize their time with Jesus? What are your own experiences? If you are honest with yourself, you may have left and come back. How many times?

The Miraculous Draught of Fishes

Twelfth Encounter with Saint Joseph

All: We adore You, O Christ and we praise You! Because by the Wood of the Cross and the Light of the Resurrection, You have redeemed the world!

Reading: *At just after daybreak, Jesus stood on the beach, but the disciples did not know that it was Jesus. Jesus said to them, "Children, you have no fish, have you?" They answered him, "No." He said to them, "Cast the net to the right side of the boat, and you will find some." So they cast it, and now they were not able to haul it in because there were so many fish. That disciple whom Jesus loved said to Peter, "It is the Lord!" When Simon Peter heard that it was the Lord, he put on some clothes, for he was naked, and jumped into the sea. But the other disciples came in the boat, dragging the net full of fish, for they were not far from the land, only about a hundred yards off.* (John 21:4-9)

Saint Joseph: Witnessing Jesus as an adult was beautiful for me. I am joyful to have been able to observe Him in His youth and now from heaven for eternity. Hearing Him call someone Children during His Resurrection let me understand He consumed what I taught Him about being human. He combined his human compassion, mercy, and love with His Divine counterparts to make both greater than the sum of the parts. God has given you the ability to combine your humanity and Divinity for others. Letting Divinity become part of who you are takes effort and practice. I am here anytime you want to pray with me.

Saint Peter Alerted by Saint John to the Presence of the Lord Casts Himself into the Water by James Tissot[13]

Prayer: Saint Joseph, lover of God and neighbor, pray with us. In Jesus' name, Amen.

Meditation Technique: Open Your Bible to a Random Page

Our Bibles can be an important tool to use for meditation. If you open a page where the overall content does not seem meditative, locate a small phrase or word instead. Once you decide what you will use, let what catches your attention become what you think about relative to your relationship with God for a few moments. Doing this pulls you away from distractions and helps you concentrate and focus on God. These thoughts can be quite relaxing and prepare you for a faith-filled discussion.

---

[13] James Tissot (Nantes, France, 1836–1902, Chenecey-Buillon, France). *Saint Peter Alerted by Saint John to the Presence of the Lord Casts Himself into the Water (Saint Pierre averti par Saint Jean que le Seigneur est là se jette à l'eau)*, 1886-1894. Opaque watercolor over graphite on gray wove paper, Image: 6 5/16 x 9 in. (16 x 22.9 cm). Brooklyn Museum, Purchased by public subscription, 00.159.344 (Photo: Brooklyn Museum, 00.159.344_PS2.jpg)

Discussion Group Scenario:

We have all had choices when we have decided not to continue something. Other times, we persevered with the results of sometimes not being as successful as we would have liked. However, those times when we tried multiple times and succeeded, stayed with us and encouraged us to continue doing the same. Looking back, can you see a relationship between prayer and success? How about those times when you felt Jesus's presence during decisions to keep trying? How did you feel in those times, whether successful or not?

The Risen Lord Eats with the Disciples on the Shore of Tiberias

Thirteenth Encounter with Saint Joseph

All: We adore You, O Christ, and we praise You! Because by the Wood of the Cross and the Light of the Resurrection, You have redeemed the world!

Reading: *Jesus said to them, 'Bring some of the fish you just caught.' So Simon Peter went over and dragged the net ashore full of one hundred fifty-three large fish. Even though there were so many, the net was not torn. Jesus said to them, 'Come, have breakfast.' And none of His disciples dared to ask Him, 'Who are You?' because they realized it was the Lord.* (John 21: 10-12 - NRSVRE).

Saint Joseph: My Son, Jesus Christ, opened the gates of heaven. In Glory, He challenges His friends to help prepare people to go through the gates. Jesus gave them an example of how working together could lift the heavy, close-to-breaking net onto the shore. He is with them glorified, with us as the body of Christ, sharing His nourishing love to fill the net to the breaking point. His community, Church, and presence can fill you to overflowing if you allow it. It is food for your soul and for you to share with the many who do not know where to find Him.

The Second Miraculous Draft of Fish by James Tissot[14]

Prayer: Saint Joseph, guide to heaven's riches, pray with us. In Jesus' name, Amen.

Meditation Technique: Reduce Information Processing

If you have a job or enormous task that includes the need to use technology, you probably have that close to the front of your mind. Just mentioning technology brings it to the surface. You may have to make a call first thing in the morning. Perhaps you have a looming deadline, or you have to have a conversation with someone that you do not want to have. The key to this technique is to convince yourself that you will have time to do it later. God wants to talk to you now through those who are with you. God and those with you deserve your full attention. Your mind will let it go so your heart can take over.

---

[14] James Tissot (French, 1836-1902). THE SECOND MIRACULOUS DRAUGHT OF FISHES (LA SECONDE PÊCHE MIRACULEUSE), 1886-1894. Opaque watercolor over graphite on gray wove paper, Image: 6 1/8 x 10 in. (15.6 x 25.4 cm). Brooklyn Museum, Purchased by public subscription, 00.159.345 (Photo: Brooklyn Museum, 00.159.345_PS2.jpg) - https://www.brooklynmuseum.org/opencollection/objects/4616

Discussion Group Scenario:

You may have felt you cannot explain how you got through something. Those of you who have given birth know this feeling of how our human body can handle such enormous change. Think about the specific instance of how the net did not break when maybe it should have because it held so many fish. Isn't it possible Jesus was there with love in a miracle like the way that the fish held within the basket, fed thousands? Couldn't that be explained by Christ's love? Think back to your situations that seemed impossible. Was Jesus with you?

The Risen Lord Forgives Peter and Entrusts Him to Feed His Sheep

Fourteenth Encounter with Saint Joseph

All: We adore You, O Christ, and we praise You! Because by the Wood of the Cross and the Light of the Resurrection, You have redeemed the world!

Reading: *When they had finished breakfast, Jesus said to Simon Peter, 'Simon, son of John, do you love Me more than these?'... Peter was distressed that Jesus had said to him a third time, 'Do you love Me?' and he said to Him, 'Lord, You know everything, You know that I love You.' Jesus said to him, 'Feed my sheep.... Follow Me.'* (John 21: 15, 17b, 19b)

Saint Joseph: I was certainly upset at my Son for assuming He could stay behind in Jerusalem, but after confronting him, He became closer to Mary and me. In a single instant, all was forgiven. Remarkable graces and love flowed like never before. Jesus is this way with all His friends. Even with Peter's, with your denial, all Jesus asks from you is to climb the mountain of His love. Yes, Jesus, I love you as a friend. Yes, Jesus, I love you as a brother. Yes, Jesus, I love you as you love me. It is here, at the top, at the edge of heaven, that I can greet you. Here, all is forgiven, all Graces flow, all love feeds His sheep.

71

Feed My Lambs by James Tissot[15]

Prayer: Saint Joseph, obedient and trusting father, pray with us. In Jesus' name, Amen.

Meditation technique: Relaxed and Comfortable Body Position
Some of you may know there are forms of yoga that can be meditative. Unlike other forms of meditation, it is physical. These brief meditations before the discussion period are meant to take a minute, so yoga is not practical. However, even with yoga, there is a routine to do a little stretching beforehand. You may have been sitting for a while, so stand up and stretch any way you can. While you do that, think of the most relaxed, restful, and comfortable position you could be in. Let that thought help your body relax. Hold onto that thought as you sit back down for the discussion.

---

[15] James Tissot (French, 1836-1902). FEED MY LAMBS (PAIS MES BREBIS), 1886-1894. Opaque watercolor over graphite on gray woven paper, Image: 9 5/8 x 6 3/8 in. (24.4 x 16.2 cm). Brooklyn Museum, Purchased by public subscription, 00.159.347 (Photo: Brooklyn Museum, 00.159.347_PS2.jpg) - https://www.brooklynmuseum.org/opencollection/objects/13529

Discussion Group Scenario:

Forgiveness is a critical part of being a Christian. Without the ability to forgive, we are not whole, as our humanity and Spirit are not united as Jesus has taught us. Jesus gives us an extreme example of Peter being forgiven for the three denials. Jesus gives him a chance to flush away the past by letting Peter understand forgiveness as an action of love. Jesus matches the times of denial and enforces within Peter's mind the power of love. Think about when you have forgiven. Did it take time? Did you wrestle with whether you should do so or not? Did you need multiple confirmations or confrontations with the person you needed to forgive? In the end, was there forgiveness, or is it still not flushed from your heart?

The Risen Lord Sends the Disciples into the World

Fifteenth Encounter with Saint Joseph

All: We adore You, O Christ, and we praise You! Because by the Wood of the Cross and the Light of the Resurrection, You have redeemed the world!

Reading: *Go therefore, and make disciples of all the nations, baptizing them in the name of the Father, and of the Son, and of the Holy Spirit, teaching them to observe all that I have commanded you. And behold, I am with you always, until the end of the age.* (Matthew 28: 19-20)

Saint Joseph: Allow me to enter your thoughts fully, so we can be together, heart to heart, soul to soul. Climb with me, as my Son did, to love's most incredible heights. From these peaks, we can see the span of humanity. Listen to the groans of a world seeking what is missing in their lives. You know the path here, the truth, the answer. Trinity is eternally yours. Go be with them, like my beautiful wife, full of Grace. They need to know your joy and to know Christ's love.

75

The Lord's Prayer by James Tissot[16]

Prayer: Saint Joseph, full of Christ's love, pray with us. In Jesus' name, Amen

Meditation Technique: Reduce but Do Not Ignore Your Senses

With everything going on in your life and worldly events, your mind and heart can be overwhelmed. Being overwhelmed in mostly seeing and hearing can physiologically affect our other senses. For instance, our sense of pain lets us know we have a headache from stress. When we are out of sorts from what is happening in our lives, it is challenging to give time to God. Jesus knows and understands because He had to deal with all these same issues. We know Jesus would go someplace silent to pray. If you can, become silent and let Jesus's love wash over you. Ask Jesus to hold the overwhelming internal feelings and physical issues at bay for a little while. Even just this thought should let you know Jesus has your back.

---

[16] James Tissot (French, 1836-1902). THE LORD'S PRAYER (LE "PATER NOSTER"), 1886-1896. Opaque watercolor over graphite on gray wove paper, Image: 8 1/2 x 6 7/16 in. (21.6 x 16.4 cm). Brooklyn Museum, Purchased by public subscription, 00.159.167 (Photo: Brooklyn Museum, 00.159.167_PS1.jpg)

Discussion Group Scenario:

In what is known as the great commissioning, Christ sends the disciples into the world, so others can know the Good News. Obviously, this was not the end of the commissioning Jesus has done or will do. We are all commissioned to be present for each other humbly and to help show others the signs of Jesus's love. Our commissioning is unique and individual to us, with endless possibilities. Some are called to have our family be our ministry. Others are called to discern greater tasks than God is asking of them. Can you give examples of each from the present time? Are they people close to you or more public figures? Are you willing to share what you believe is your commission?

The Risen Lord Ascends into Heaven

Sixteenth Encounter with Saint Joseph

All: We adore You, O Christ, and we praise You! Because by the Wood of the Cross and the Light of the Resurrection, You have redeemed the world!

Reading: *When they had gathered together, they asked him, 'Lord, are you at this time going to restore the kingdom of Israel?' He answered them, 'It is not for you to know the times or seasons that the Father has established by His own authority. But you will receive power when the Holy Spirit comes upon you, and you will be my witnesses in Jerusalem, throughout Judea and Samaria, and to the ends of the earth.' When he had said this, as they were looking on, he was lifted up, and a cloud took him from their sight.* (Acts 1:6-9)

Saint Joseph: We are in the presence of each other, a communion of souls. We have transcended human limitations to get here. You have risen towards me, and I have come toward you. Like you do now, I watched my Son reach heaven many times in His humanity. His ascent is continual because He is the Alpha and the Omega. He may have risen from your sight yet consider that your faith has unveiled His presence.

79

The Ascension by James Tissot[17]

Prayer: Saint Joseph, human teacher to Jesus, pray with us. In Jesus' name, Amen.

Meditation Technique: Remembering an Intense Non-Romantic Love Scene

My mother had gotten confirmation that she was going to pass from cancer very soon. I had rarely heard her speak of love or say *I love you* very often. She was always uncomfortable with any emotion, so I never said anything to her. In one of our last calls, before she passed out of nowhere, she said, "I love you." I was stunned, and for a few moments, I was speechless, but I also told her I loved her. I have witnessed this in other people in my ministry role, so I should have been saying it myself, yet I was unprepared for it. It is still one of my top outpourings of extremely intense unconditional non-romantic love almost twenty years later. This was a key to using this kind of love in meditation to get to a quiet place. Perhaps you have a memory like it to go to your special place.

---

[17] James Tissot (French, 1836-1902). *The Ascension (L'Ascension)*, 1886-1894. Opaque watercolor over graphite on gray wove paper, Image: 9 7/8 x 5 13/16 in. (25.1 x 14.8 cm). Brooklyn Museum, Purchased by public subscription, 00.159.348 (Photo: Brooklyn Museum, 00.159.348_PS1.jpg) https://www.brooklynmuseum.org/opencollection/objects/13530

Discussion Group Scenario:

You are filled with the power of the Holy Spirit. What does this unique gift of the Holy Spirit's availability mean to you? Is this power only available when you ask? Is it possible that some of the holy people in your life can turn to the Spirit? Is someone in the group willing to share an experience that directly happened, or they witnessed when there was no doubt that the power of the Holy Spirit was present?

Mary and the Disciples Keep Vigil in the Upper Room

Seventeenth Encounter with Saint Joseph

All: We adore You, O Christ, and we praise You! Because by the Wood of the Cross and the Light of the Resurrection, You have redeemed the world!

Reading: *When they entered the city, they went to the upper room where they were staying.... The apostles devoted themselves with one accord to prayer, together with some women, and Mary, the mother of Jesus, and His brothers. Suddenly there came from the sky a noise like a strong driving wind, and it filled the entire house in which they were. Then there appeared to them tongues as of fire, which parted and came to rest on each one of them.* (Acts 1:13a, 14 and Acts 2:2a-3)

Saint Joseph: Pray with me, Mary, my holy wife, and our Lord's friends in joyful prayer. God has poured Himself out upon us. We are filled with His Spirit. It surrounds us, calms us, brings us peace, and fills us with hope, faith, and love. Listen to the whispers of God's will in the wind. To know this gift of Spirit is always to know joy and love because He is always with us.

83

The Descent of the Spirit, engraving by Gustave Doré [18]

Prayer: Saint Joseph, full of joy, pray with us. In Jesus' name, Amen.

Meditation Technique: Reimagining

What or where is your favorite place to be when you want to be alone with the Lord? What can you remember from it? Is there a scene, maybe a certain amount of light or calming sound? Is it in the quiet of your mind and the warmth of your heart? Imagine you are there right now. What do you see, touch or smell? Why does it evoke such a warmth of being with the Lord for you? Let your thoughts wander about this solitary place. Can you put yourself in spirit there right now even though you are not actually there? If so, you have found a wonderful meditation technique to get you quickly to calm and peace.

---

[18] The Bible panorama, or The Holy Scriptures in picture and story by Foster, William A., 1891, Collection from The Library of Congress
(https://archive.org/details/biblepanoramaorh00fost/page/n3/mode/2up)

Discussion Group Scenario:

We often see or perceive phenomena that may or may not be real. Does that make it any less important if God is part of it? Great poets and artists often attempt to describe or shape something they have lived. They cannot even adequately describe something they have participated in. We can turn to the book of Revelation to see how John is doing his best to use human words and conditions to give us some idea of what is happening. When you read or see works like this, do you focus on the human traits used to convey the phenomena? If not, do you still believe what allows you to do so without the human elements? Is it okay to change the focus from the phenomena God presented from human to spiritual thought?

In the Presence of Christ

Eighteenth Encounter with Saint Joseph

Reading: *While they were eating, Jesus took bread, gave thanks and broke it, and gave it to his disciples, saying, "Take and eat; this is my body." Then he took the cup, gave thanks and offered it to them, saying, "Drink from it, all of you. This is my blood of the covenant, which is poured out for many for the forgiveness of sins. I tell you, I will not drink of this fruit of the vine from now on until that day when I drink it anew with you in my Father's kingdom.* (Matthew 26:26-29)

Saint Joseph: We have shared a journey with the Risen Lord. As servants and witnesses of Christ, let us now pray how our Savior taught us.

All: Our Father, Who art in heaven, hallowed be Thy name. Thy kingdom come, Thy will be done on earth as it is in heaven. Give us this day our daily bread, and forgive us our trespasses, as we forgive those who trespass against us. And lead us not into temptation but deliver us from evil. For thine is the Kingdom, and the Power, and the Glory forever, Amen.

The Communion of the Apostles by James J. Tissot[19]

Prayer: Let us offer each other a Sign of Peace. In Jesus' name, Amen,

Meditation Technique: Open Your Bible to a Random Page

Open your Bible in a slightly less random way to a book that you seldom look at. For many, it is the book of *Revelation* because of all the fire and brimstone. Randomly pick out something in your chosen book, even if what is being said is challenging. Look at it as a way to remind you of something that is going on in your life or the world. What would you say or do if you could change what you read as it relates to what it reminded you of? God is listening for what is in your heart. God wants to hear what you say how you feel, as you likely have made it a positive view with your Christian viewpoint. Breathe in and hold onto the comfort you sense from knowing God knows how you feel.

---

[19] James Tissot (French, 1836-1902). THE COMMUNION OF THE APOSTLES (LA COMMUNION DES APÔTRES), 1886-1894. Opaque watercolor over graphite on gray wove paper, Image: 9 7/16 x 13 1/2 in. (24 x 34.3 cm). Brooklyn Museum, Purchased by public subscription, 00.159.223 (Photo: Brooklyn Museum, 00.159.223_PS1.jpg) https://www.brooklynmuseum.org/opencollection/objects/13470

Discussion Group Scenario:

In the journey of the Resurrection with words, painting, and fictitious conversation with Joseph, you have had the opportunity to explore creative ways to view Jesus in multiple dimensions. Does this approach interfere with the way you have known? Does it conflict with how your pastor teaches? Do you have any reservations about adding incremental ways to get closer to God? What is your takeaway from this experience?

How have you changed during this journey?

Draw yourself showing the before and the after.

ABOUT THE AUTHOR

Jerry is a happily married practicing Catholic living in Central Massachusetts (New England, USA). He is actively involved in a variety of both being- and doing- ministries. To be present to God and others by waiting is a difficult challenge, as it is his nature to react by finding solutions to every problem immediately. His attempts to do so would not be possible if he did not take time for prayer. His life experiences far outweigh his computer technology, graduate business, and pastoral ministry degrees. His observation is that his education in knowing the language of business and personal beliefs, along with his doubting Thomas within, appropriately mingles the human and divine nature of who he is. He has found that he quickly burns out, attempting to fight every wrong he observes.

Jerry has realized that his specific commission means he must responsibly identify and use his God-given gifts. He tries to share his belief in the love of God and neighbor as appropriately as possible, especially knowing he has a choice in accepting God's will. Jerry loves writing about the ordinary times of God's peace, love, and actions. He firmly believes we can tap into an internal desire to know unconditional love.

Jerry appreciates and understands that what he writes can be radically different from the belief of others as he does lean on his experiences and background of practicing his faith. He firmly believes that your faith can help shape you into someone willing to be kind and compassionate. He only asks that, as he does for you, that you regulate your reaction to his writings by accepting another person's belief that has the commonality for all that "God is love."

Other Books by Jerry Francis (available through Amazon)

Although by Night - Daily Lectio Divina, 2018

The Living Flame of Love – Daily Lectio Divina, 2019

Ephphatha, That is, Be Opened! – Daily Lectio Divina, 2020

Without Love, I am Nothing – Daily Lectio Divina, 2021

Daily Gospel Reflections using Lectio Divina for the 2023 Liturgical Calendar

Daily Gospel Reflections using Lectio Divina for the 2024 Liturgical Calendar

The following works by Jerry are or will be published through *ShelteringTree.Earth, LLC*.

For the Good of the Order

https://www.amazon.com/Good-Order-Jerry-Francis/dp/1946469629/

Book Trailer: **https://youtu.be/N6UleR0h-RA**

Scriptural Rosary Mysteries for Thriving (Alternate Rosary bead mysteries)

Dipsaō - I Thirst

The Kingdom of Heaven is Like a Merchant Searching for Fine Pearls

Chanterelles in The Garden

The Color of My Heart

A Moment for Christ

Also – each year we will be adding a new *Via Lucis* from the perspective of other saints and apostles. Click the Amazon link for the series! Reserve your copies now on ShelteringTreeMedia.com

Our books will help you feed His sheep.

Visit **SheleringTreeMedia.com** for more information.

Made in United States
Troutdale, OR
02/25/2024

17973121R00058